Celebrations

Happy Mother's Day!

Erin Day

PowerKiDS press

New York

Published in 2017 by The Rosen Publishing Group, Inc.
29 East 21st Street, New York, NY 10010

First Edition

Managing Editor: Nathalie Beullens-Maoui
Editor: Melissa Raé Shofner
Book Design: Michael Flynn
Illustrator: Continuum Content Solutions

Library of Congress Cataloging-in-Publication Data

Names: Day, Erin, 1986- author.
Title: Happy mother's day! / Erin Day.
Description: New York : PowerKids Press, [2017] | Series: Celebrations |
   Includes index.
Identifiers: LCCN 2016027218| ISBN 9781499427653 (pbk. book) | ISBN
   9781499426700 (6 pack) | ISBN 9781499429497 (library bound book)
Subjects: LCSH: Mother's Day–Juvenile literature.
Classification: LCC HQ759.2 .D39 2017 | DDC 394.2628–dc23
LC record available at https://lccn.loc.gov/2016027218

Manufactured in the United States of America

CPSIA Compliance Information: Batch #BW17PK: For Further Information contact Rosen Publishing, New York, New York at 1-800-237-9932

Contents

Today is Mother's Day!

4

I made my
mom a card.

My mom loves the outdoors.

She likes to hike and
go to the beach.

Today, my mom wants to go to the park. I pick flowers for her.

We see an ice cream cart.
My mom likes strawberry
ice cream best.

My dad spreads out
a big blanket.

We all sit down to
enjoy our treats.

The sky is filled with fluffy white clouds.

I see a turtle
float by. My mom
sees a shark.

We take a walk around
the duck pond.

16

My mom holds my
hand so I don't fall in.

I have an idea on the
way home. I will make
my mom a gift.

I use bright beads
to make a necklace.
My mom loves it!

She gives me a big hug.
The best part of Mother's Day is
spending it with Mom!

Words to Know

flowers

necklace

pond

Index